Published by Dial Books for Young Readers, A division of Penguin Putnam Inc. 345 Hudson Street, New York, New York 10014. Text copyright © 2002 by Alice B. McGinty. Illustrations copyright © 2002 by Melissa Sweet. All rights reserved. Designed by Lily Malcom. The text for this book is set in Cafeteria. Printed in Hong Kong on acid-free paper. Library of Congress Cataloging-in-Publication Data•McGinty, Alice B. Ten little lambs / Alice B. McGinty ; illustrated by Melissa Sweet. p. cm. Summary: As they play all through the night, "little lambs" from ten to one finally fall asleep. ISBN 0-8037-2596-5 [1. Sheep—Fiction. 2. Sleep—Fiction. 3. Night—Fiction. 4. Counting. 5. Stories in rhyme.] I. Sweet, Melissa, ill. II. Title. PZ8.3.M1585 Te 2002 [E]—dc21 00-063875
10 9 8 7 6 5 4 3 2 1

The artwork was created using watercolor and color pencils on Arches hot-pressed paper.

To Jake and Zachary with all my love
—A.B.M.

For Mark
—M.S.

Ten Little Lambs

Alice B. McGinty

illustrated by Melissa Sweet

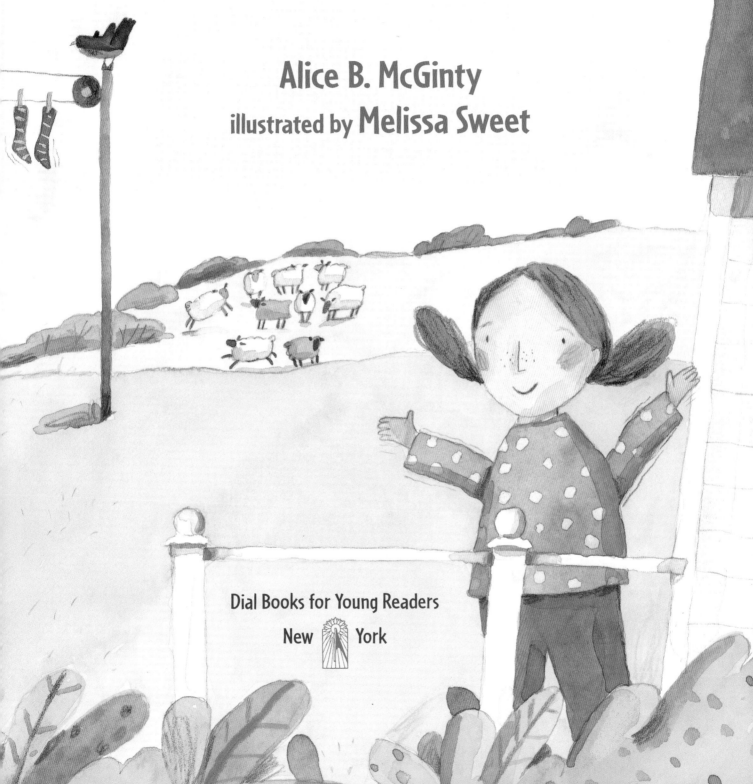

Dial Books for Young Readers

New York

Good night, little lambs.
Go to sleep.

Ten little lambs who won't go to sleep.
What will they do all night?
They'll tackle and tumble, and wrestle and rumble.
Ten little lambs, all night.

Nine little lambs who won't go to sleep.
What will they do all night?
With pleasure they'll pour all their toys on the floor.
Nine little lambs, all night.

Eight little lambs who won't go to sleep.
What will they do all night?
They'll pile their bedding in mountains for sledding.
Eight little lambs, all night.

Seven little lambs who won't go to sleep.
What will they do all night?
They'll launch seven pairs of high-flying bears.
Seven little lambs, all night.

Six little lambs who won't go to sleep.
What will they do all night?
They'll plow winding freeways through piles of pj's.
Six little lambs, all night.

Five little lambs who won't go to sleep.
What will they do all night?
They'll build a skyscraper with oatmeal and paper.
Five little lambs, all night.

Four little lambs who won't go to sleep.
What will they do all night?
They'll go out exploring to see who is snoring.
Four little lambs, all night.

Three little lambs who won't go to sleep.
What will they do all night?
They'll tell riddles and tales of pirates and whales.
Three little lambs, all night.

Two little lambs who won't go to sleep.
What will they do all night?
They'll paint swirling oceans with lipsticks and lotions.
Two little lambs, all night.

One little lamb who won't go to sleep.
What will she do all night?
She'll look long at the moon and hope day will come soon.
One little lamb, all night.

Ten little lambs, at last all asleep.
What will they do all night?
Those smiles are a warning.
They're dreaming of morning.